TANGLED TAPESTRY

*A Collection of
19 Western Short Stories*

by James J. Huble

TANGLED TAPESTRY
A Collection of 19 Western Short Stories
by James J. Huble

©2016 James J. Huble
ISBN# 978-1-939345-07-3
Library of Congress Control Number: 2016943286

First Printing August 2016

Published by
Goose Flats Publishing
P.O. Box 813
Tombstone, Arizona, 85638
www.gooseflats.com

All rights reserved. No portion of this book may be reproduced or transmitted in any form by any means, electronic or mechanical, including photocopying, recording, scanning to a computer disk, or by any information storage and retrieval system, without express permission in writing from the author and/or publisher. All characters appearing in this work are fictitious. Any resemblance to real persons, living or dead, is purely coincidental and unintentional.

DEDICATION

For my wife, Sandy,
and my sons, Ted and Pete

What tangled tapestry we weave
As we spin the yarns that we conceive
James Huble

Contents

GUNMAN'S LEGACY - 1

SWIFT JUSTICE - 7

SMOKE - 13

GOLD - 21

TOO MANY, TOO EASY - 25

VANISHING MAN - 29

DOMINION - 39

THE PERFECT CRIME - 43

DOGGONIT - 49

THE INHERITANCE - 57

TRAGIC PRICE - 61

LAST HUNT - 69

SAN FRANCISCO - 73

MANY SHAPES - 77

THE LONG SHOT - 81

ONE GOOD TURN - 87

MUSICAL RENDERINGS - 95

LEGERDEMAIN - 99

PRINTS - 105

GUNMAN'S LEGACY

It was early evening when Mitch Tanner rode into Corinth. The town appeared to be a sleepy little place. Just what he was looking for. With luck, maybe he could stay a little while. With luck. He was tired of moving from town to town.

He thought he had found some peace and quite in the last small town. Webbsville. Then he had to kill a man. He wasn't running from the law. It was clearly self defense. It was always self defense. Some slick gun that wanted to prove he was faster than Mitch Tanner. So then he'd have to move on to the next place. Why couldn't they just leave him alone?

He considered drawing too slow a couple of times, but instinct just took over. He tried changing his name, but somebody always came along and recognized him, so he gave up on that idea. Funny thing was, Mitch Tanner wasn't even his real name. It was a name he took fifteen years ago.

Well, he'd give Corinth a try. All he needed was a little luck.

He dismounted in front of "Ma's Home Cookin" and entered. The waitress, a pretty young blonde, brought him a menu, and poured a cup of coffee.

"What do you recommend?" Mitch asked.

The waitress smiled and answered, "The beef stew. 'Cause that's all we got left."

Mitch glanced over the menu carefully and then grinning said, "I'll have the beef stew."

"Comin' right up," laughed the young blonde.

Mitch studied the other patrons in the dining room as he drank his coffee. The waitress set a steaming plate of stew on the table, and refilled his cup.

"Thanks," he said. "What time do you serve breakfast?"

"Six thirty, if you want to beat the crowd."

Mitch laughed. There were only four tables that he could see. "How big is the crowd?"

Her eyes sparkled mischievously as she replied, "Don't be silly," humming as she walked away.

Mitch chuckled. This just might be the place, he thought. He stood, placed a silver dollar on the table, and went in search of a rooming house.

Corinth proved to be an easy going community. Mitch was accepted by everyone readily, though he tended to keep a low profile. The name, Mitch

Tanner, didn't appear to mean anything special to anyone living in Corinth. A couple of months had gone by, and he was still leading the life of a normal citizen. He took on a few odd jobs to pay his meager expenses until he was able to get more steady employment as a clerk in Bob Wilson's general store. It looked like 'Lady Luck' had finally smiled on him. He didn't even wear a gun when he was working in the store.

The wind was cold on the gloomy, cloudy afternoon that turned bitter for Mitch. He had been taking a leisurely ride on the outskirts of town when the weather suddenly changed from bright sunny to dismal grey. And when he rode into Corinth he found that the atmosphere was even more dark and grim.

"Mitch Tanner, I've come to kill you." The words were shouted from across the street, slightly behind him.

Mitch froze in the saddle.

"Dammit," he muttered. He slid off the bay he was riding and stepped around the horse to face his challenger. "Good God," he exclaimed. It was just a kid. Barely old enough to maybe have peach fuzz.

Mitch stared at the kid in shocked amazement. "You sure ya really wanna do this boy?"

The youngster made no reply. His eyes blazed in defiance, but the rest of him showed hesitation.

"You think you're a fast gun, boy? You tryin' ta make a name for yourself by killin' Mitch Tanner?"

"No I ain't," stammered the boy. "That ain't why." The answer came as a complete surprise to Mitch.

"Then what in hell are you doing, bracin' me like this?" shouted Mitch.

"Ma said it was your gun that killed my Pa. I come to even the score."

"Who was your Pa, boy?"

"Matt Turner. He was Matt Turner." The youngster seemed close to tears as he said the name.

The boy's words struck Mitch like a cold steel club. He went ridged for a moment.

"Ruth Ann told you that did she? Yeah, that would be her way," he said quietly.

"You said Ruth Ann," exclaimed the boy. "Did you know my Ma?"

Mitch nodded. "Yes, I did. She's the most beautiful woman I ever seen. How is she?"

"Ma died this past June. I buried her and then come lookin' for you," said the boy. "I aim ta kill you."

Gunman's Legacy

"I ain't goin' ta pull against you, boy." Mitch unbuckled his gun belt, and dropped the rig on the ground at his feet. "I don't think you're the kind to shoot me when I'm unarmed. I trust you never killed any others before you jumped me. I sure don't want to start you down a gunslinger's path."

"I'm truly sorry about your Ma, boy," said Matt Turner as he mounted his horse and rode out of Corinth.

SWIFT JUSTICE

The Silver Creek Bank had been robbed at 9:00 am that morning. By 10:30 am the trial was under way.

Stanley Elliot had arrived in town only yesterday. He had planned on opening a law office in Silver Creek, hoping to establish a clientele. He now suddenly found himself defending the accused.

The bank was owned by the town's most influential citizen. A man that Elliot had heard referred to as Colonel. Stanley didn't know if this was a rank earned during the Civil War, or was only an honorary title.

The man accused of the crime, Elliot learned, was an annoying enemy of the Colonel's. They had once been partners in a ranch outside of Silver Creek. A ranch which was now owned solely by the Colonel.

Frank Sibley had sworn that he had been cheated out his share of the ranch two years ago. The Colonel had tried to drive Sibley out of the area by various means, but the man remained a thorn in the Colonel's side. This hasty trial now provided the perfect chance to achieve what the Colonel desired.

Stanley Elliot had intended only to be a spectator at these very hurriedly assembled proceedings. He found it amazing how quickly things were put together. The Colonel had simply called some names and these men now comprised the jury.

Two men testified how the bank robber had shot the teller and ran from the bank with a bag of money. They followed him outside, and saw him turn into the nearby alley. They ran into the alley where they apprehended Frank Sibley.

As the Colonel spoke to the jury about the necessity of swift justice, Stanley Elliot stood, cleared his throat and interrupted.

"My name is Stanley Elliot," he began. "I'm an attorney at law." He paused for this statement to register.

"It doesn't appear that Mister Sibley is here. Shouldn't he be allowed to present some defense?" asked Elliot.

The Colonel glared at Stanley. "I'm afraid Mister Sibley is in no condition to make an appearance. He is too drunk to walk."

"Isn't there someone who can speak on his behalf?" inquired Elliot.

"How long have you been in Silver Creek, Sir?" asked the Colonel.

"I only arrived yesterday," replied Elliot.

"I see," responded the Colonel. "Have you been present throughout the trial as it has advanced so far?"

"Yes, I have."

"Then you have heard all of the testimony. If you would care represent Mister Sibley, you may do so," said the Colonel with a smug expression.

"It was not my intention to become a part of the proceedings," responded Elliot.

"However, you have expressed a regard about the defendant's rights. If you are genuinely concerned, act now, or forever hold your tongue." The Colonel turned toward the jury and smiled arrogantly.

"Very well," replied Elliot. He took a few moments to compose himself and then spoke. "You said Mister Sibley was too drunk to attend this trial. Has he been drinking while in custody?"

"No, Sir! Not in my jail!" shouted the sheriff.

"Thank you," said Elliot. Looking at the men who had chased the robber, he continued, "You said the man ran from the bank. Did he run fast?"

The two men answered in unison. "You bet. Very fast!" One of the men added, "He had long legs."

"Long legs? He was tall then?" asked Elliot.

"Yeah, six feet or maybe a little more."

"I see," muttered Elliot. He paused. "What did you do with the money?" he then asked.

"What money?" asked one of the men with a confused expression.

"The bag of money taken from the bank by the robber," answered Elliot. The two men exchanged glances.

"We didn't do anything with it. We didn't find any money."

"No money, hmm," smiled Elliot. "How tall do you think Frank Sibley is?"

"He's about my size," said one of the men. "Around 5 feet 10."

"Let me see if I've got things right," said Elliot. "The man who robbed the bank was at least 6 feet tall. Sibley is about 5 feet 10."

"Sibley apparently didn't have the bag of money, or you would have found it when he was apprehended." Another pause.

"The man who robbed the bank ran very fast. But Sibley... who is now very drunk... and has not been drinking while in custody... must have been very drunk when he was caught." With great emphasis Elliot continued.

"As he is now, too drunk to walk."

Swift Justice

Elliot paused for effect and then asked, "So how could he **run** from the bank?"

Stanley Elliot stepped over in front of the jury. "Do these facts lead to the belief that Frank Sibley is the thief who robbed the bank?"

"You have made a most clever presentation, Sir," said the Colonel staring at Stanley Elliot. "I hope you are now satisfied that Mister Sibley's case has been adequately stated."

The Colonel slowly turned to the jury. With a grand display of cultivated polish he pontificated, "My good gentlemen of the jury. You know your duty. Please execute it promptly as expected!"

The men of the jury looked at one another and nodded. One man stood and hung his head for a moment. Then he looked up and announced, "We find the defendant guilty!"

Stanley Elliot's jaw dropped open in absolute staggering astonishment.

"Swift Justice, Sir. Yes! In Silver Creek.... Swift Justice prevails. Colonel Nathan B. Swift, your humble servant."

SMOKE

Ted Murphy watched as the Wells Fargo Stage rattled into Douglas. Ted was the foreman of the Circle T Ranch located in the nearby hills. That was rolling country, but it had good grass and water, so Ben Mason had chosen to raise his cattle there.

Mason lived on the ranch with his wife Nellie and his daughter Charlotte. Charlotte was the reason Ted Murphy was in town. Ben Mason had asked Ted to escort his lovely daughter into Douglas so that she could buy a few things that Nellie and Charlotte wanted.

Ted and Charlotte were walking back to their buggy when the stage arrived. They both stopped as a tall, well dressed, handsome man stepped from the stage. A very soft gasp came from the girl as she gazed at the man, obviously attracted to him.

Although the sound of the gasp was low, it was still heard, and caused the man to look at Charlotte. He smiled and advanced toward her. He removed his Stetson hat and bowed graciously. "Clyde Bennet, your servant," he said quietly.

Charlotte was flattered. She smiled and, offering her hand, batted her eyes. Bennet, a twinkle in his eye, took her hand and brushed his lips across the back of it with a display of gallantry.

Ted Murphy was seething. Still he managed to control his anger. Charlotte was openly flirting with this stranger. She was his girl. At least that's what he thought. He expected she would marry him as soon as he had finished building the log house out under the big oak tree near Mason's home. Ben and Nellie Mason already treated Ted as their son.

Ted tried to gently guide Charlotte over to the buggy, but she resisted. He didn't want to make a scene, so he just quietly said, "We should be getting back to the ranch."

Clyde Bennet quickly intervened. "Oh, do you have to leave so soon? I was hoping you would have dinner with me."

Ted Murphy was flabbergasted when Charlotte responded, "I would simply delight in having dinner with such a handsome and charming gentleman." And that was the start of a blossoming relationship.

Clyde Bennet simply swept Charlotte Mason off her feet. He called on her at the Mason ranch, and bedazzled Ben and Nellie also with stories of his exploits. He said he had come from San Francisco

Smoke

where he had several business ventures, and was now considering investing in cattle.

Ted Murphy was disgusted. Not just because Charlotte no longer seemed to be interested in him, but because he didn't trust Bennet. Clyde was just too smooth. Too slick!

Ted was expressing his sentiments to Molly Perkins over apple pie and coffee at Molly's café. "Would you like some more pie?" asked waitress Mary Woods sweetly. Mary had always had a crush on Ted, but he didn't seem to notice her.

"No thanks," replied Ted. "A little more coffee would be nice." Mary scooted away and rushed back with the coffee pot.

"You shouldn't be down on yourself, Ted," remarked Molly. "Charlotte doesn't know what a mistake she's made passin' you up. Why, any woman with any sense would choose you over that slippery talkin' dude. Isn't that right Mary?"

Blushing, Mary Woods turned away and hurriedly carried the coffee pot back to the nearby counter.

"Maybe I should marry you, Molly," chuckled Ted.

"Nah, your much too old fer me," laughed the fifty year old lady.

"I wish I knew more about this fella," said Ted. "Maybe I'll just have ta make some inquiries."

Within a month of the arrival of Clyde Bennet in Douglas, a wedding date was set. The church was filled to capacity by the townsfolk and nearby ranchers.

The bride looked beautiful in her long flowing white dress as she walked down the church aisle with her father, who was almost strutting, he was so proud.

The couple to be married now stood in front of the preacher as he said, "If anyone has any reason why this man and woman should not be wed, let them speak now, or forever remain silent."

At that moment a lady sitting in a wheelchair entered the back of the church and called out, "I have reason!"

"Who might you be, madam?" asked the preacher.

"Why, I'm Clyde's wife."

The gasps were overwhelmingly loud. Clyde spun about. "What the hell?" he hollered.

Charlotte stared at the woman in the wheelchair. She slapped Clyde's face and ran from the church sobbing.

"Wait," cried out Clyde.

Ben Mason glared at Clyde and shouted, "You rotten scoundrel!" Then he and Nellie stormed out of the church.

Smoke

The congregation sat in awkward stunned silence.

The lady in the wheelchair calmly said, "I'll be in room four at the hotel. You can find me there." Then she in her wheel chair was pushed out of the church by the man who was with her.

Clyde stood in disbelief, unable to speak. Shaking his head as he left the church, he walked down the street to the hotel, and climbed the stairs to room four. He didn't bother to knock, just opened the door and barged in.

The woman was no longer sitting in the wheelchair. She now stood by the window smoking a slim cigar. The man who had been accompanying her was seated on the bed.

"Who the hell are you?" snarled Clyde.

"Why, Clyde honey, I'm your wife. Didn't you hear me over in the church?" said the woman chuckling.

"I never saw you before in my life," barked Clyde. "What are you trying to pull?"

"I'm pullin' your strings, Honey. I got a paper here called a marriage certificate that says you and me are man and wife."

"That's impossible," sputtered Clyde.

"Anything is possible when you got a man as clever as Frank here is with pen and ink."

"So what kind of swindle are you up to? And what's with the wheelchair?" asked Clyde.

The woman laughed. "The chair was to immediately get the sympathy of everybody in the church. Nice touch, right?" She smiled. "Now, for five thousand dollars, we can have our marriage annulled."

"You've got to be kidding," laughed Clyde. "You can't annul a marriage that never took place. Why would I pay you to have that done anyway? You've already messed up my real wedding plans."

"Your right," said Frank, who until now had said nothing. "But for five thousand dollars, we can set things straight with the bride and her family. We will tell them it was a case of mistaken identity"

"For five thousand dollars, hunh?"

"Sure, a man of your means should be able to spare five thousand dollars in order to marry the girl of his dreams."

Clyde started to laugh. Just a chuckle at first that developed into a genuine belly shaker. He was laughing so hard his eyes started to water.

"I hope you two chumps haven't invested too much time and money in this farce," said Clyde still laughing. Then he composed himself and stated,

"I couldn't give you **five** dollars, let alone five thousand, even if I wanted to."

"What about all those business ventures in San Francisco?" asked Frank.

"Pure smoke," answered Clyde. "Just part of the build-up so I could marry Charlotte Mason and get a foot in the door at Mason's cattle ranch."

The woman stubbed out her cigar in an ashtray on the bed-stand. Looking at Frank she said, "Well, I guess that's about all we need to know. We can give our written report to Ted Murphy and be on our way back to the agency."

The woman smiled at Clyde Bennet and drolled, "A little smoke screen of our own to uncover a cheap, two bit four flusher."

Stunned, Bennet stared at the woman. "Damn," he exploded. Then more softly, but with emphasis, "Damn...Damn...Damn!"

He clenched and unclenched his fists several times, while standing ridged in silence. Then he turned abruptly and left the room.

It was a flustered and frustrated Clyde Bennet that left Douglas the next day. Ted Murphy was on hand to watch him board the stage. Bennet stopped beside the coach long enough to glare at

Ted. Murphy smiled and touched the brim of his black flat crowned hat just before Clyde climbed in.

Ted Murphy was apologetic when he handed the investigator's report to Ben Mason. "I just couldn't stand by and see Charlotte get taken in by that conniving cur."

"Oh, Ted," squealed Charlotte as she threw her arms around him. "I'm so sorry. I guess I really learned a lesson."

"I guess we both did, Charlotte. I see now that expecting you to marry me was a mistake. I ain't never going to be rich and refined like you thought Clyde Bennet was."

Ted paused for a moment. "I need a wife who is satisfied with just me. So I asked Mary Woods to marry me, and she said: Yes!"

GOLD

Cass Winslow sat in a leather chair behind a fine mahogany desk in his office smoking a big cigar. Cass was owner of the Longhorn Saloon. Across from him sat Luther Mitchell.

Luther was the present owner of the Bitter Creek Mine. Luther purchased this mine from Winslow several months ago for five hundred dollars. He had been laboring in the mine ever since without striking the vein of gold that had been contemplated. When he bought the mine, Cass Winslow had promised he would buy it back if Luther failed to hit pay dirt. That's what the two men were now discussing.

"I'll give you two hundred dollars," said Winslow.

"But I paid five hundred, and you said you would buy it back," pleaded Mitchell.

"And I will make good on that promise," said Winslow. "But I didn't say I would give you back five hundred. I'm willing to pay what I think it's now worth."

Luther Mitchell squirmed and sputtered, "But you led me to believe that was the deal."

"I'm sorry you thought that," said Cass smiling. "But there was never any agreement like that stated." Winslow took a puff on his cigar.

"Well, it don't seem fair to me," griped Mitchell.

"Before I sold you the mine, we both saw signs of gold, didn't we?" Winslow knew for certain that was the case. He had salted the Bitter Creek with just enough traces to spark the interest of any potential buyer.

"Yeah, I guess that's so," replied Mitchell. "But except for what we saw then, I ain't found any more. None at all."

"Yes, well that is indeed most unfortunate. But that's exactly why the Bitter Creek isn't worth more than two hundred to me." Cass placed his cigar in a silver tray on the desk. He leaned back in his chair and smiled.

"That's my offer, Luther. Take it or leave it. It's up to you."

Luther Mitchell grumbled. "I don't think it's fair, but it don't make sense to keep on diggin', so I guess I'll take the two hundred."

After Luther Mitchell left his office, Cass Winslow broke out laughing. The Bitter Creek and been a 'gold mine' for him. Not that there was ever found any actual gold. But he had sold the mine and bought it back like just now so many times that he had made a very substantial profit.

Gold

Cass had originally obtained the Bitter Creek by cheating Jeremiah Hatch in a poker game when the old miner had been drunk. Jeremiah had found color and even a number of nuggets that indicated there might be a payload. That had attracted Cass Winslow's attention.

Winslow picked away at the mine rock walls for a short time without finding any gold. He didn't like getting his hands and clothes dirty, so he gave that up, deciding to sell the Bitter Creek. In desperation to rid himself of the mine, he had told the buyer he would buy it back if requested. Of course Cass never had any intention to honor that promise.

But when that first unhappy buyer insisted he keep his word, Cass became suddenly inspired. He saw a possibility for a clever scheme, and it had certainly paid off.

Well, now he would once again salt the mine with just enough traces of gold to stir the interest of the next sucker. And he didn't have long to wait.

Orville Harvey came into the Longhorn shortly after arriving in town. While he was sipping his beer, he overheard Cass Winslow talking to one of the bartenders about the Bitter Creek Mine. Cass had made sure that this conversation would be picked up by Harvey.

The next day Harvey approached Winslow about the mine, and Cass was only too happy to show him what appeared to be a potential gold strike.

As before, he promised to buy it back if Harvey was unsuccessful.

A few months went by, and like all the other men who had tried and failed in the Bitter Creek venture, Orville Harvey sat in Cass Winslow's office discussing their deal.

Just as before, Cass said, "I'll give you two hundred dollars."

And again, like all the others, Orville Harvey protested. And like all the others, he grumbled and took the two hundred.

But Orville Harvey was not a man to be trifled with. He was a vengeful man, who felt that Cass Winslow had swindled him. After making inquiries, and learning that Winslow had made many similar dealings in the past, Harvey decided to put an end to such dirty conniving.

Late one night Harvey snuck out to the Bitter Creek and set dynamite charges. He placed explosives in the entrance and also several sticks in the cave that had been dug out over the years.

Harvey watched from a safe distance as the charges went off and the Bitter Creek Mine was blown into a shambles of broken rock, sealing the entrance. What he didn't see, nor anyone else ever saw, was the internal fissure that was created by the blast. There exposed was the brightest wall of gleaming gold anyone could imagine.

TOO MANY, TOO EASY

Jenks Jarvis had been wandering footloose without direction since the end of the Civil War. Lots of men found themselves drifting around aimlessly after that terrible conflict.

He had fought on the "right" side. Alas, it had been the losing side. Jenks referred to it as "The War Between The States". That seemed more fitting because it was anything but "civil".

Then he decided he would start mavericking. There were plenty of unbranded cows in the washes and coulees along the Brazos. So, with a rope and a running iron he managed to build a small herd of wild, range cattle.

It was rough and dirty work. Sometimes dangerous, since those Texas longhorns were big and ornery mean. Many a cowpoke had been injured or killed in a careless moment.

After gathering thirty head, enough to get started in the cattle business, but not so many he couldn't handle them alone, he drove them West out of Texas. Along the way, Jenks picked up a few stragglers from other herds crossing the open range. By the time he got into New Mexico his bunch numbered close to fifty He found some good grazing land that had a clear creek, and started ranching.

Jenks still had his rope and running iron, so he helped the herd grow by branding what he called stray calves. He figured it was just like what he did back in Texas. Maybe they weren't really wild, or even orphaned, but why be particular. They didn't have a brand, so he put one on them. And he also added to the herd by making a few clever purchases of cattle driven through the territory. Jenks never questioned any of the cowboys he bought cows from regarding their origin. He rationalized that after all he had driven a bunch over from Texas. How was this any different?

The herd prospered, and after a couple of years, Jenks now had about fifteen hundred head. He was quite proud of the way he had achieved this with minimal expense. Yes, a smart man could really be successful in the cattle business. And he was smart.

Jenks saw no reason to discontinue the practices that led to his success. So when the opportunity arose to acquire another one hundred steers at less than half of what they were worth, he jumped at the chance. He winked at the cowboys who signed a bill of sale.

It was two or three weeks later that Jenks noticed some of his cattle acting strangely. Several seemed to be very unsteady on their feet, and a few were lying down and didn't seem to be able to stand.

An examination by the New Mexico Territory Veterinarian disclosed a crisis. Jenks' entire herd was quarantined and then would have to be destroyed. That last clever deal had included more than he had bargained for. His whole herd now had anthrax.

James Huble

VANISHING MAN

The stage from Bisbee rolled into Tucson without much fanfare, stopping in front of the "Grande Parlor House" hotel. The trip had been routine and uneventful. Passengers exiting included a smartly dressed business man and his wife, a drummer wearing a gaudy catalogue suit beneath a dusty bowler hat, and a slim, lanky cowboy, neatly dressed but ordinary in appearance.

The business man and wife entered the hotel. The drummer, carrying his satchel, headed for the "Copper Palace" saloon. The cowboy paid a visit to the local sheriff, and introduced himself. Arizona Ranger, Clint Adams.

"I'm here investigating the where-a-bouts of a certain Henry Kimble," explained Adams. "He's the brother of Frank Kimble, a rancher outside of Bisbee. Frank received a telegram from his brother stating that Henry had liquidated his business interests in Los Angeles, and would be arriving in Bisbee three days ago. But he didn't show."

"So, you want me to make some inquiries?" asked Sheriff Pat Tilman.

"No," replied Clint. "I'm just letting you know what I'm doing here. I'd rather look into this myself. And I'd appreciate it if you didn't say anything."

"Well, saying nothing and doing less is the easiest part of my job, but if you decide you need any help, just holler," chuckled Tilman.

Clint Adams exited the sheriff's office and strolled down to the "Grand Parlor House". "You have a fellow by the name of Henry Kimble stay here some time in the last few days?" he asked the clerk on duty.

"Who wants ta know?" was the testy reply.

Clint smiled. "He's a friend of mine. I was supposed to meet him, but I got delayed. Maybe he spoke of me. I'm Clint Adams."

"Na, he never mentioned you."

"Then he was staying here."

"What?...ah...Yah, guess he was," mumbled the clerk.

"When was that? How long did he stay?" asked the ranger.

"Well..."The clerk fumbled with the hotel registration book. Finally flipping a couple of pages, he pointed out, "He was here just the one night. Checked in last Thursday, checked out Friday morning."

Clint nodded. "Thanks." He started to leave, and then turned back. "He say anything about where he was going?"

The clerk seemed more willing to respond. "Ya know...I remember now. Big fella with red hair and a full beard. Said he was takin' the train for Los Angeles. Left here 'bout the same time as Lily Fremont. I think they knew each other. Least wise, she knew him. Called him by name."

"You say 'Los Angeles'?" replied Clint.

"Yes, Sir. And Miss Fremont said that was where she was goin' too, so they could travel together,"

Clint left the hotel pondering. Why would Kimble take the train to Los Angeles, when he had just come from there?

And a second puzzle. Why didn't he send his brother, Frank, another telegram about his change in plans?

The next stop for Clint Adams was the train station. The station master, a short, barrel chested man of around fifty, recalled seeing a red headed man with a full beard boarding the train for Los Angeles a couple of days ago. "He and Miss Fremont got on the train right after they loaded a big crate on the east bound stage coach", he said.

"When does the train run?" asked Clint.

"The West bound leaves Tucson in the mornin'. The East bound arrives in the evenin'," replied the station master. "Be in around five."

While he waited for the evening train, Clint pondered some more on his two puzzles. And he also added a third. Since Kimble and the girl where on their way to Los Angeles by train, why did they send a big crate in the opposite direction by stage?

With nothing better to do until the train came, Clint decided to mosey over to the Wells Fargo stage office. There he asked the stage line manager if he remembered anything about the big crate that was placed on board a couple of days ago.

The manager, a middle aged man with a handle bar mustache and twinkle in his eye, said, "Yes siree, Sonny. That was a mighty big wooden crate. Not sometin' I'm likely ta fergit."

"Do you recall where it was going?" asked Clint.

"Not right off. I could look it up. But it don't make no difference, 'cause it never got there anyway."

"Never got there?" said Clint in surprise.

"Nope. Ya see that stage was held up. A lone robber stole the crate, along with some other packages." Chuckling he added, "Must a been a real hassle ta lug somthin' that big on horseback."

Clint thanked the manager for the information and stepped out of the Wells Fargo office. Then he heard train pulling in to Tucson, so he hurried over to the station. He decided he would talk to the train conductor.

"A big man with red hair and full beard? Sure I remember him. It's only been a couple of days. I ain't lost my memory yet," snorted the conductor. "'Sides he was with Lily Freemont. I sure don't fergit a pretty woman like her."

"Do you happen to recall his name?" asked Clint.

"Well, now let me think. Seems I recollect Miss Fremont calling him Henry somethin'. That was after they was seated and we was under way."

"And they got off in Los Angeles?" inquired Clint.

"Not both of them," the conductor replied. "Miss Fremont got off in Yuma, along with some other fella she met on the train. I never seen him get on." The conductor paused and stared off into space for a moment, and then remarked, "Ya know, I don't recollect ever seeing the big red haired man get off the train."

"He didn't leave the train in Los Angles?" asked Clint.

"No, I'm sure of that. He musta got off some where though, 'cause he sure ain't still on the train." There was another pause. "Matter of fact I don't 'member him on the train after Yuma. But I know he didn't get off there."

The conductor now had a bewildered look, as Clint stood contemplating what he had just heard. The conductor was a very observant man, and he was right when he said Henry Kimble was not still on the train. But he also said that he never saw Kimble leave the train.

Clint was really baffled. He was sure that somewhere in this jumble of information there was a key to the where-a-bouts of Henry Kimble. He wasn't still on the train, but he didn't get off. He didn't get off, but he wasn't seen after Yuma. Clint complimented the conductor on his observation skill and memory, thanked him for the information, and left the train station.

Turning these thoughts over and over in his mind, Clint pondered. How could someone not get off the train, and not still be on the train?

Then it hit him. Of course. The only logical explanation for these conflicting contradictory facts was...Henry Kimble never got on the train!

Clint was certain that his guessing was correct. Then he added another thought to his list of significant facts. Lily Fremont didn't go to Los Angeles like she said. She got off in Yuma. Why? And who was the man that got off with her?

Clint decided that he had to find Lily Fremont. He needed her to answer some questions. He was certain she was the key to this. But he really didn't have anything to hang his hat on to make her cooperate.

Then he remembered about that big crate. Clint wondered what became of it, and what was in it?

Vanishing Man

The next morning Clint returned to Sheriff Tilman's office to ask him about the stage holdup. Learning where the robbery had taken place, and that the crate had been found smashed and empty nearby, Clint decided to rent a horse, and ride out to the sight and look around. Since he was investigating a matter different than the holdup itself, he thought there might be some clue that would mean something to him, that might be overlooked by the sheriff.

Arriving at the holdup sight, Clint easily found the crate. Smashed as described. But a very careful inspection of the pieces revealed a couple of interesting details. Some fabric torn from a man's suit was caught on a small nail attached to one of the boards. And that fabric contained several red hairs. Clint frowned when he examined them.

Henry Kimble had been in this crate. Clint was sure of it. A wealthy man kidnapped perhaps. But more than likely dead.

Convinced that the stage robber would not want to carry a body very far, riding in ever widening circles, Clint searched the area for signs of a grave. It took him about an hour to locate some recently turned soil. And as he had guessed, he found Henry Kimble buried. He never got on that train. Somebody had been impersonating him long enough to make it look like he had gone back to Los Angles. And Lily Fremont was in it up to her lovely neck.

Tracking down Lily Fremont was easier than Clint Adams had expected. He learned that she had returned to Tucson, and was staying at the "Grande Parlor House."

Further questioning of the hotel clerk revealed that he had not been on duty when Henry Kimble checked into the establishment, but had learned of his description from the night duty clerk. So when a man with red hair and a full beard presented himself to check out, he had no reason to doubt his identity. And especially when Miss Fremont called him by name.

Clint then confronted Lily Fremont in her room at the hotel. He identified himself, presenting his Ranger's badge. "You're under arrest for murder," he stated sharply.

Lily Fremont was so frightened that in exchange for leniency, she agreed to give testimony against her accomplices. The man she claimed had planned and executed the major parts of the crime was also staying at the hotel.

"I met him sometime ago when we were both members of a theatre group. He used various disguises at different times, and we swindled several wealthy men," she said matter of factly.

"And murder was just part of the game?" remarked Clint.

"Oh, No!" she answered with alarm. "Never before!

Miles Thornton, that's his name, said it was an accident. He put the body into an old theatrical wardrobe crate. He told me I had to go along like always, or we'd both hang."

She explained that once on the train, Thornton had simply stepped out onto the rear platform of the last coach, removed a red wig and false beard, and placed them, along with the suit coat he was wearing, in a valise that she had been carrying. In Yuma the two of them got off the train. Just like that Henry Kimble had vanished.

"The night clerk, Jeremy Butts, was part of it too," she added. "He helped us by giving the day clerk Kimble's description. And he was the robber of the stagecoach."

Clint escorted Lily Fremont to the Tucson jail, and then he and Sheriff Tilman rounded up Miles Thornton and Jeremy Butts.

Clint Adams had found Henry Kimble, but it was a bitter triumph. He made his report in Tombstone to Ranger Captain John Jackson, and was thankful that it was not his job to break the sorrowful news to Frank Kimble.

James Huble

DOMINION

Ben Taylor watched the big stallion race across the flats in the Catalina foothills. Coal black, shining like oil in the afternoon sun, the horse was indeed a magnificent creature.

Ben had been trying to catch this wild mustang for several months, but the horse was just too clever to fall for the many tricks that Ben had tried. Tricks that had often succeeded with other wild horses continually failed with this cunning devil.

Ben had built temporary corrals around the few water holes he knew of in the area, but the big mustang must have found water somewhere else. Ben had tried luring him into roping range by pasturing a few mares in likely places, but that didn't work either.

Removing his well stained Stetson, Ben scratched the top of his head. He saw the stallion drop out of sight into a wash leading into Rainbow Gorge. He waited patiently for the mustang to reappear, and when he didn't, Ben's heart almost stopped in anxiety. He couldn't imagine such luck.

Rainbow Gorge was a blind canyon, only one way in or out. Surely the big black stallion was aware of this. If Ben could get to the entrance before the mustang came back out, he'd have that black devil trapped long enough to get a rope on him.

Ben spurred his buckskin gelding into a fast gallop toward the wash. He was so exited he didn't even feel the slapping of brush and branches as he raced onward. He slowed his horse to a comfortable trot as he approached the entrance to Rainbow Gorge. Uncoiling his rope lariat in preparation for the anticipated moment when he would confront the big stallion, he rounded the first curve in the canyon wall.

The wild mustang stood defiantly facing Ben in the middle of the canyon floor. Ben reined his buckskin sharply and started his rope. The next events happened so rapidly, that everything seemed to be a blur.

First there was a snarl and awful scream, and then a huge tawny form struck Ben, knocking him out of his saddle. He hit the ground with a stunning thump. His arms were numb and helpless, and he became aware of a pair of blazing yellow eyes, and the awfulness of sudden death.

And then the big black stallion hurled forward. Rearing high on his haunches, he crashed down on stiff forelegs time after time until the great mountain lion lay dead. Then the mustang rose one more time on his haunches. This time he came down stiff legged straddling a flabbergasted Ben Taylor.

Dominion

The big stallion snorted once, and then slowly walked out of Rainbow Gorge. A King in his Dominion.

James Huble

THE PERFECT CRIME

Saul Bigalow slid open the big front door of his livery stable. Rambling, he muttered unintelligibly as he began his morning routine. With small shuffling steps he approached the stalls intending to fork some hay to the horses. His gnarled hands stopped in midair as he reached for the pitchfork. He squinted and rubbed his eyes, struggling to clearly focus on something hanging from the rafters at the dark end of the building. When recognition came, Saul whirled and ran as fast as his old legs could manage, heading straight for Sheriff Mark Hanlin"s office.

As Sheriff Hanlin followed Saul back to the livery stable, a few curious residents of Junction City joined the pair. Arriving at the building, Hanlin ordered the group to remain outside. Then he walked to the rear of the stable and confirmed what Saul had told him. The body of Nathan Caruthers was hanging from the rafters, a noose around the neck.

Hanlin called to a couple of the men outside to assist him. After removing the noose, they carefully lowered the body and carried it to the mortician's office for further examination.

The cause of death seemed evident. There was no sign of a struggle. But why would a prominent, successful man such as Nathan Caruthers commit suicide? Also, there was nothing there, like a box or a chair, for Caruthers to jump from, so then, how could he hang himself?

To add to the mystery, examining the body revealed a freshly branded mark. What resembled skull and crossbones had been burned on Caruthers' neck.

Junction City was a beehive of speculation about Caruthers'death. But no answers were forthcoming. The significance of the skull and crossbones was completely baffling.

Because of the several unusual factors involved, Sheriff Hanlin was investigating this death as a possible murder. However, not to alarm the citizens of Junction City, he went about his inquiries discreetly.

Two weeks later a second body was found in the livery stable. This time it was Foster Benjamin who was hanging from a noose. And he, too, was burned on the neck with skull and crossbones. Now Sheriff Hanlin was certain of murder.

Foster Benjamin and Nathan Caruthers had been two of the four founding fathers of Junction City. The other two, Jason Redford and Thomas Townsend were considerably concerned. Was some disgruntled madman from the past suddenly taking revenge on these wealthy businessmen?

The Perfect Crime

Sheriff Hanlin assured the two prominent citizens that he was taking these deaths very seriously and investigating thoroughly and rapidly. But as days, and then weeks, went by, the sheriff uncovered nothing. He could find no one with a motive for these killings.

A month had passed when Jason Redford visited Thomas Townsend late at night. Townsend let his friend in and offered him a drink.

Jason, I asked you to come here tonight to talk about the hangings." Townsend crossed to a chair and sat down. He motioned for Redford to take a chair also.

"Who do you think might be responsible for hanging Nathan and Foster?" asked Townsend.

"I have no idea," replied Redford.

"Are you worried that you might also be an intended victim? Have you taken any steps to protect yourself?" asked Townsend.

Redford looked a bit surprised. "Of course I have some concerns, but I'm not frightened," he said. "I haven't started carrying a weapon if that's what you're suggesting."

Townsend stood and refilled Redford's glass. "Maybe you should," he remarked. He returned to his chair and sat.

"The four of us did some conniving and somewhat questionable deeds while acquiring our wealth and prominent positions. We scuttled the law on more than one occasion." Townsend paused. "Have you thought any about what the skull and crossbones brand on the necks of Benjamin and Caruthers might mean?"

"To be honest, I haven't," replied Redford. "I've left the investigating to Sheriff Hanlin."

Townsend laughed sarcastically. "That rube will never figure it out. We were all pirates, don't you see? We commandeered anything and everything in sight."

Redford stared in confusion at Townsend. "What the hell...are you...talking...about?" His speech started faltering and his eyes blurred.

Townsend laughed again. "Your drink was drugged, Jason. I'm going to brand you and hang you, just like the others."

"Bbb...but...wh...why? What... do you...gain?"

"Most of the schemes we pulled off were my ideas. The three of you went along and reaped the profits."

Townsend grumbled. "Well, when I was in Tucson a couple of months ago, I consulted with a doctor about some pains I was having. It turns out I have a cancer that will kill me soon."

The Perfect Crime

Townsend laughed hysterically. "Think of it, Jason. My schemes. And I won't be around to benefit. Well, neither will any of you." His high pitched laughter filled the room.

Townsend stood and walked over to Redford. "They'll find you hanging in the livery stable just like the others. And then in a couple of weeks, they'll find me branded and hanging there also. And they'll never figure it out. The Perfect Crime."

James Huble

DOGGONIT!

"Git otta my yard!" snarled Homer Baynes. "You dern kids stay away from here. An take thet goldang mongrel dog with ya!" Shaking his fist and grumbling, he shouted, "I musta told ya a hunnerd times. Stay otta my yard!"

The four youngsters ran away laughing. One of them turned and stuck out his tongue. Then he called to the dog, "Camon, Rufus. Old grouch Baynes don't want us 'round his place."

The four boys didn't really have any special reason to play in Homer Baynes' yard except that they knew it made him mad, and it was fun to make him come out of his house and holler. And Rufus had a great time digging in the old man's garden.

"What are ya hollern about now, Homer?" called Sarah Baynes as her husband came into the house, slamming the back door.

"Oh, them blasted kids was playin' in the backyard agin. An thet goldang dog a theirs was diggin' in the garden. One a these days I'm gonna shoot thet little devil!"

"Homer, don't you dare shoot that dog," said Mrs. Baynes reproachfully. "Them boys ain't hurtin' a thing, and that garden you make such a fuss about ain't nothing but weeds."

"Well, iffin the dang dog wasn't diggin' in there all the time, maybe somethin' else would grow," muttered Homer.

"You ain't put no seed in there for a couple of years, and you know it," retorted Sarah.

"There ain't no sense in putting seed in there when it's just gonna be dug up," answered Homer. "An ifin I don't want them boys in my backyard, then they should stay out." Looking sternly at his wife he snapped, "And you shouldn't be takin' their side agin me!"

"Land sake, Homer, seems you always got somethin' ta complain about. Besides, them boys is just makin' fun of you. The more you holler, the more they come around here."

"I just told ya, don't be takin' their side. I don't much care fer yer naggin'!"

A few weeks later Homer Baynes stopped his buckboard in front of the Bisbee post office. He went inside and checked to see if he had any mail. Then he told Saul Stein, the postal clerk, that he was going to Tombstone for a couple of days, and asked Saul to hold his mail 'till he got back.

Three days later Homer Baynes hurried into Sheriff Ben Morgan's office. He appeared so agitated that he could hardly speak. Waving a piece of paper that he held he sputtered, "Ben, ya gotta help me."

Sheriff Morgan looked up. "What's wrong, Homer?" he asked startled. Baynes looked like he was having a heart attack.

"Here." Homer thrust the paper at the sheriff. Morgan took the paper and read.

> We got your wife. If you want to see her alive again, put $500 in a bag, and drop the bag under the tall pine tree up on Goose Flats Butte. Don't tell the sheriff or anybody else.

The letters were cut out of some periodical and pasted on to the paper.

Baynes stammered, "I been in Tombstone fer the last couple days. When I got home I found this note. What am I gonna do?" Ben.

Morgan stood and stepped over to Baynes. Taking Homer by the arm, he led him to a nearby chair.

"What em I gonna do, Ben? I ain't got five hunnerd dollars."

Trying to comfort Baynes, Sheriff Morgan quietly said, "Relax, Homer. Take a deep breath. It won't do any good for you to panic and have a stroke."

Baynes hung his head and buried his face in his hands.

"Now don't worry, Homer," said Morgan calmly. He took a parfleche from his desk drawer. "I'll set a trap for these kidnappers. I'll put a bunch of cut up newspapers in this bag, and you take it up to that big pine. Me and my deputy will keep watch and we'll catch 'em. Don't you worry."

Homer did as the sheriff advised. A couple of days later Homer was in the sheriff's office again. This time he was angry as well as upset. "I tried yer dang blasted idée. It didn't work. Lookit this." He threw the parfleche bag, along with another note, onto the sheriff's desk.

You shouldn't have told the sheriff. You got one more chance. Get it right.

Doggonit

"Now don't bust a gut, Homer. That didn't work. We'll just have to try something else," said Morgan calmly.

"I'd pay ifin I could. But where in hell do I get five hunnerd dollars?"

"I'll talk to some of the town leaders. I'll ask them to take up a collection. We will raise the money for you and get Sarah back."

A few days later Baynes carried the parfleche bag with $500 dollars in it up to Goose Flats Butte, and placed it under the big pine tree as stated in the first note. For the next week, Morgan or his deputy, Frank Moseby, kept watch day and night. It was during a rain storm that the bag disappeared. But Sarah Baynes remained missing.

Homer Baynes became extremely despondent. He told everyone it was his fault, because he had gone to the sheriff right away. The townsfolk tried to calm his grief but to no apparent avail. Homer turned away from everyone and became a recluse. For a couple of months the only time anyone saw him was when he bought supplies. Then suddenly he announced that he was going to sell his place and go away.

The four boys were in his backyard again. Homer burst out the back door. "Git otta here!" he shouted. "Dammit!"

The dog had been digging in the garden again and now was carrying something in his mouth. Homer stormed into his kitchen and grabbed his shotgun, but by the time he was back outside the boys and the dog were gone.

"What ya got there, Rufus?" asked one of the boys as he scratched the dog's ears. The boy saw it was a parfleche bag. As he was taking the bag from the dog's mouth, Sheriff Morgan was walking by. He glanced at the boy and dog and then stopped in his tracks.

"Can I see that bag?" asked Morgan.

The boy gave the parfleche to the sheriff, who studied it carefully for a moment. "Where did you get this?" inquired Morgan.

"Rufus dug it up in old man Baynes' garden."

"I'll need to keep this for a while," said the sheriff. Hurrying back to his office, he asked Frank Moseby to get a couple of shovels and follow him.

They entered the backyard at Homer Baynes' place, and begin shoveling where the dog had been digging. The first thing uncovered was a ladies shoe. Then they found what they suspected was buried there.

Homer Baynes stepped out of his back door and saw what the two men were doing. He howled, "I knew I shoulda shot thet goldang mongrel dog!"

Doggonit

THE INHERITANCE

The Bar Double X ranch was a prosperous cattle operation. Mathew Carlton, the owner, didn't really know much about cows, but he was an excellent administrator. Carlton relied on his foreman, Milt Harris to deal with the everyday working of the ranch.

Carlton lived on the ranch with his wife, Anna, and his twin sons, Christopher and Jeffrey. He adored his wife, so it was a real tragedy when Anna contracted scarlet fever and died. The twins were twelve years old.

Carlton, though not harsh, had been a somewhat distant and strict father. Now that Anna was gone, he seemed further removed from the boys. He spent most of his time alone his study, either going over the ranch records, or reading one of the many books resting on the shelves along the study walls.

Chris and Jeff were left pretty much on their own. They ate in the kitchen with the cook, Carlotta. They were expected to do certain chores around the ranch. As they grew older, taller, and stronger their duties became more demanding.

The twins now spent most of their time with the ranch hands, doing much the same work. Carlton never thanked the boys nor praised them for their diligent efforts. Jeff seemed to just take things in stride, but Chris became very resentful.

On paydays the boys received wages much the same as any ranch hand. Jeff accepted the money cheerfully, but Chris always grumbled that it wasn't enough. "After all," he said, "We're the boss's sons. Why can't the old man cough up a little extra for his own sons?"

As time went by, Chris found a way to make a little extra money. He began selling off some smaller items he gathered around the ranch house. A couple of valuable rings that had belonged to his mother, a pair of silver candlesticks collecting dust on the fireplace mantel, a small painting that was almost completely hidden behind some miscellaneous clutter. He was sure his father would never miss them, since he didn't pay much attention to anything outside his study.

Chris wasn't sure if Jeff had any idea of what he was doing. But since nothing was said about it he wasn't going to worry.

As time went by Chris took several more pieces of his mother's jewelry, and two small figurines that were made of gold. And since his activities in this pursuit were apparently unnoticed he continued to walk off with any items of value that were easily carried and could be quickly converted to cash.

The Inheritance

Late one evening while sitting in the big easy chair in his study Mathew Carlton had a massive heart attack. When Carlotta entered the study the next morning to bring Mathew his breakfast, she found him dead.

Because he had been somewhat reclusive these past few years, the daily operations of the ranch were not interrupted by Carlton's death. Milt Harris continued as always to handle the cattle business. Carlotta as always prepared the meals for everyone. Jeff took the responsibility of arranging for his father's funeral. Chris eagerly conferred with the family attorney, Malcolm Wilson, to set a date for the reading of the will.

Malcolm Wilson gathered those persons mentioned in the will. He now stood before them in Carlton's study. He began reading, "I Mathew Carlton, being of sound mind and rational thinking...."

Chris suddenly interrupted, "Never mind all that fancy introduction. Just get to the meat of the old man's will."

Carlotta gasped and Milt Harris cleared his throat loudly. Jeff stared at his brother.

"Yes, well let me see," stammered Wilson.

"To my faithful housekeeper and cook, Carlotta, I give all of the fine china and silverware along with five hundred dollars."

Wilson continued, "Milt Harris is to have at his choice any five horses in my stable, excluding my personal mount 'Butternut', along with five hundred dollars."

Wilson turned to the twins.

"The land, the buildings, and the remaining live stock are to be shared equally by my sons, Christopher and Jeffrey."

Wilson detached a page from the will and continued reading. "The addendum which is titled 'Christopher' is to be given to him. In it I bequeath certain specific items. All other possessions not previously specified shall be bequeathed to Jeffery."

Malcolm Wilson gave Christopher the document mentioned. Chris snatched the page from Wilson's hand and very anxiously began reading. His jaw dropped open. He was stunned. He couldn't believe his eyes.

It was an itemized list of all the things he had stolen through out the years.

TRAGIC PRICE

Colonel Barton C. Langdon sat at his desk in Fort Humphrey listening with eagerness to the report Pony Stealer, his Crow chief of scouts, was making. If what the scout was saying was accurate, it could mean there would be some peaceful days ahead, and a boost to his career.

"Black Eagle has decided to talk about bringing his band of Apaches into the post reservation," explained Pony Stealer.

"He said in three days you are to come with only two pony soldiers carrying a white flag. He will have two warriors with him at Canyon Springs."

"How did you learn of this," asked Colonel Langdon.

"Black Eagle told me this himself. He appeared suddenly surprising me as I was returning to the fort this morning." The scout spoke with little expression.

"And you believe him," asked Langdon.

"Yes. He does not lie. Certainly he could have killed me," replied the Crow.

Colonel Langdon stood excitedly. "Of course I'll be there. And you will accompany me and Sergeant Harris. You will act as our interpreter."

"I will come with you," replied the scout, "But you will not need me to interpret. Black Eagle speaks your language better than most white men."

"Well, that is a surprise. I didn't realize that. How does he come to know English?"

"He went to Santa Maria Mission School until he was ten years old. The padres taught him English as well as religion. He speaks Spanish also."

"What happened?" inquired the stunned colonel. "Was he stolen by the Apaches?"

"Not exactly. His father, Spotted Cat, simply came to the mission when his mother died, and took him away. It was she that wanted the boy to be schooled by the padres."

"He's been a cunning adversary. I'll be anxious to meet with him. Do you think he will really bring his band to the reservation?"

Pony Stealer just shrugged and said nothing.

"I guess we'll find out in three days," said Colonel Langdon smiling at the scout.

Pony Stealer's passive face revealed nothing as he again shrugged.

Three days later, Colonel Langdon waited with Sergeant Harris and Pony Stealer at Canyon Springs. Langdon thought Black Eagle had chosen the meeting place wisely. The desert dust and high temperature made for a deep appreciation of the spring water.

Langdon was wiping his brow with a wet kerchief when Black Eagle rode up. True to his word, the Apache had brought only two warriors with him.

Colonel Langdon gazed at the Apache leader with astonishment. Black Eagle was much younger than Langdon had expected. Probably late twenties, at most early thirties. And he was strikingly handsome.

The three Indians dismounted. The colonel had always considered himself as fit and trim, but this tall, muscular Apache was physically overwhelming.

Black Eagle made no attempt at any ceremonial introduction. He simply said, "You have come. Good."

Caught off guard by this short statement, Colonel Langdon wasn't sure how or what to reply. He started to offer his hand, but then withdrew it and said, "Yes, it is good we are here."

The two men stood watching each other in silence. Then Langdon spoke. "I am told that you wish to bring your people to the reservation."

"It is not my wish," said Black Eagle.

Struck dumb founded, Colonel Langdon's mouth opened in shock, but no sound came out.

"But it is something I must do for my people. We cannot survive if we go on fighting. Therefore, I have come to talk of such a move."

The colonel breathed a sigh of relief. "Yes, well I can have a treaty drawn…"

"No!" interrupted the Apache leader. "No papers. No signing. Lies put on paper are still lies. I speak from my heart. If you speak from your heart we need nothing else."

"But there are rules that must be followed at the reservation," responded Langdon.

"We will follow the rules that we agree to follow. We will also tell you some rules that you must follow." Black Eagle's eyes met Langdon's with a hypnotic gaze.

For the next two hours the leaders discussed reservation rules. Colonel Langdon felt that he was being cleverly manipulated by this Apache chief, but he was unable to resist. The chance to bring these Indians into the reservation would be a staggering achievement. A true career builder. Finally all points being settled, Black Eagle said, "I will bring my people in two days."

Tragic Price

Black Eagle rode proudly erect in front of his people as they entered Fort Humphrey. He dismounted slowly in the center of the parade ground, looked up at the flag that was waving above, walked quickly over to where Colonel Langdon was standing, and held out his hand.

Surprised by this gesture, Langdon was slow to respond. Recovering, he removed his right glove, and shook hands with Black Eagle. This simple recognition sign between two leaders was the beginning of a friendship.

For the next several months the Apaches lived peacefully at the nearby reservation. Black Eagle and Colonel Langdon met regularly. They talked often of mutual interests. Smoked an occasional cigar together. Went hiking, fishing, and hunting as companions. The bond between them became quite strong.

Colonel Langdon sat in his quarters now brooding. He wrung his hands in anxiety, rose unsteadily, and paced back and forth across the room. Then with firm decision, he slowly removed his uniform jacket and pants, exchanging them for an old pair of denims and a dismal, faded cotton shirt.

Leaving the room, he marched quickly to his office. He surveyed the room with his eyes, and then placed a letter of resignation on the desk.

Turning briskly, he walked out, hurried to the stables, saddled and mounted a horse, and rode in the evening dusk to the reservation.

It had become dark by the time Langdon arrived at the reservation. He made his way to the shelter where he expected to find Black Eagle. The Apache was sitting quietly by himself, reading a book which Langdon had given him. He looked up in surprise as the colonel entered.

Laying the book aside, Black Eagle motioned for Colonel Langdon to sit across from him. Langdon hesitated in obvious discomfort, and then finally sat without speaking.

Black Eagle had a puzzled look as he noted the colonel's clothing. "What brings you to my home this late at night? And why do you dress in this manner?" he asked.

Langdon replied solemnly. "It grieves me deeply to be here tonight. The great pain I feel in my heart is..," Langdon hung his head and seemed to be unable to continue.

Black Eagle made no sound. He watched and waited for the colonel resume speaking.

"My daughter has informed me that she is in love with you," said Langdon. "She intends to become your wife."

Tragic Price

Langdon paused. His face held a grim composure. Haltingly he began speaking again. "I ...admire you...as a man... with whom... I have... a friendship." Again Langdon paused and seemed to struggle for the next words.

"But you are an Apache... I must prevent this relationship."

Black Eagle sat calmly. "A father must follow his heart."

Langdon's chest heaved heavily as if he was unable to breath. Removing a revolver from inside his shirt he said, "There is no hatred involved. Just a deeply in-grained prejudice."

The Apache remained motionless.

"I have resigned my commission. I do not wish to bring dishonor to the United States Army or its uniform." Langdon hung his head again. Then he looked up into Black Eagle's proud handsome face.

There were tears in Langdon's eyes as he shot Black Eagle. Then he turned the revolver on himself and squeezed the trigger. A tragic price of prejudice.

LAST HUNT

Hump Pachard eased his sorrel mare down the slope. Below him in a grassy meadow he could see a small group of buffalers. That's what Hump called them, buffalers.

He had been hunting shaggy brutes like these for many years. When he first started there were huge buffalo herds and only a few hunters. Now it seemed like to be only a few buffalo, and huge herds of hunters. Was a right nasty development thought Hump.

His christened name was Phillip. Many years back he had broken his left shoulder. It never healed right, and he was left with a prominent bulge on that side. So Hump was now his moniker.

Most of the buffalo herds had already moved out of Oklahoma Indian Territory, and were making their way to winter in Ilano Estacado. But there were still some stragglers around in the first week of October.

In his younger days Hump would follow the herds into the 'staked plains'. Those were exciting times and had proved to be many an adventure. But now the aches and pains in his tired old body made a journey like that no longer practical.

Still, he figured he could make one last short hunt before laying up to rest for the winter. He didn't take a wagon, just his sorrel mare and a pack mule. He reckoned on only packing out a half dozen or so hides. Now days it was just the thrill of the hunt that mattered.

Shooting the big beasts was easy. They just milled around after the first cow was dropped. Hump picked out a couple of bulls and then another cow. When the small herd took off running, he didn't bother to give chase. He smiled at the success he had. Now came the work. He began skinning.

Hump had been so engrossed with the buffalo that he hadn't noticed the dark clouds rolling in. He had finished skinning the bulls and was starting on one of the cows when it began to rain. He wasn't eager to get wet, but he didn't figure on letting it stop him before finishing all the skinning.

Hump had just finished the last cow when a sharp bolt of lighting struck nearby. A deafening thunder boomed. In panic, the mare broke loose from her tether and raced away.

Cursing his incredibly bad luck, Hump loaded the four buffalo hides onto his mule and climbed up behind the pack.

It wasn't long before the rain turned to snow, and then icy sleet. Hump grumbled and muttered to himself, "It's too early for a storm like this." But, there wasn't much he could do except plod on.

Last Hunt

It was getting increasingly colder, and the icy sleet was making things slippery. Mules are generally sure footed animals, much more so than horses, but the overburden pack mule stumbled, slipped and went down.

Hump managed to jump clear without any injury. However, an examination of the mule's foreleg showed it was broken. Hump had no choice but to shoot the poor animal.

The temperature continued to drop and the storm was getting worse. Hump knew that trying to walk out this bad weather was out of the question. He would just have to make some kind of shelter to survive.

Pulling the pack from the dead mule, Hump started unrolling the fresh buffalo hides. He wrapped himself inside one, and then another. He wiggled up close to the soft under belly of the mule, pulled the other two fresh hides over him, closed his eyes and went to sleep.

Early the next spring, when there was only signs of a thaw, they found Hump. The fresh buffalo hides had freeze dried, and shrunk. The old buffalo hunter was rigidly encased in the shriveled skins tighter than a hook and laced corset.

SAN FRANCISCO

Norma Jean Lassiter was gazing up into the sky at the dazzling array of bright stars. "I heard San Francisco is even more glorious than a sky full of stars," she said passionately. She'd been dreaming about going to San Francisco for the past couple of years and talked about it constantly. "Will I ever get to see San Francisco, Frank? Are you really going to take me there?"

"Gee, Honey, you know I'd take you there tomorrow if I had enough money," replied Frank Murray. "After we get married, and I make my fortune, we'll go to San Francisco. I promise."

Although Frank and Norma Jean were not officially engaged, Frank always felt they had an understanding. Norma Jean proclaimed an undying love for Frank, but just wasn't ready to marry him yet.

"Do you really love me, Frank?" asked Norma Jean coquettishly, tracing her finger across his chest.

"Of course I do," answered Frank emphatically. "What kind of crazy question is that?"

"Well, if you really, really loved me, you'd find some way to take me to San Francisco."

"Gosh almighty, Norma Jean, Bisbee is a mighty long way from San Francisco. It'll take a heap of money just to pay the fare to get there. And then we'll need a lot more to stay there, even for a little while."

Norma Jean pouted. "I still say if you really loved me you could figure out some way." She laid her head against his chest. "You will find a way won't you? I know you will."

Norma Jean looked up into Frank's eyes. She kissed him on the cheek, turned away, and walked into her house, leaving him standing on the porch in a state of frustration and confusion.

It was just after supper time, two weeks later, that Frank Murray rode into the yard of the Lassiter ranch. He dismounted awkwardly, and stumbled to the side of the house where Norma Jean's window was located and rapped on it lightly.

Norma Jean walked cautiously to the window and peered out. When she saw Frank, she gasped. There was blood on his shirt just below his shoulder. She opened the window and heard him say, "I need your help. Get me over to that barn."

Norma Jean, still dressed, climbed out, and struggling with his weight, managed to assist him.

San Francisco

Once inside the barn, Frank sank down in a pile of hay.

"What happened to you, Frank?" asked Norma Jean in alarm.

"I guess I made a big mistake, Honey." He grimaced in pain. "I robbed the bank! That is I tried to rob the bank."

Norma Jean reacted in astonishment.

Frank looked up at her and tried to smile. In pain he struggled with his next words. "You said if I loved you, I'd find a way to get the money to take you to San Francisco. I got desperate thinking on it."

He grimaced as the pain stabbed in his shoulder. "I didn't reckon on taking a bullet. What's worse is I shot Mister Burnside, the banker."

Frank paused. His chest heaved in agony.

"I didn't plan on shooting him, but he pulled a gun outta the safe and then started blazing away. I guess I acted on instinct and fired back. I don't know if I killed him or not. I just ran away. Didn't even take any money."

Frank closed his eyes for a moment and struggled for breath. "You gotta hide me for a few days 'til I get enough strength to clear out."

Norma Jean starred at Frank and said, "You just stay here for now. I'll wash your wound and get something to bandage you with. I'll go into town tomorrow and find out about Mister Burnside."

The next afternoon Frank was startled out of a fitful slumber. He looked up into the muzzle of Sheriff Carl Carson's Colt .44.

"It don't look like you're about ta try anything ta get away," said the sheriff.

"But I ain't taking any chances just the same." He motioned menacingly with the colt.

Frank blinked his eyes and shook his head to clear the cobwebs in his brain. "How'd ya find me so darn quick?" he asked.

"Why, this little lady just led me right here," said Sheriff Carson pointing to Norma Jean.

Frank starred at Norma Jean in disbelief.

"For the reward, Frank." said Norma Jean coldly. "I found out in town they were offering one thousand dollars for you. I guess you finally did get me enough money to go to San Francisco."

MANY SHAPES

Living most of his thirty some years rambling across Texas and New Mexico Territory Caleb Masters had decided to venture further northwest. He traveled across Colorado and into Wyoming Territory.

Now Caleb slid quietly through the trees and brush stalking a mule deer buck. He needed to get close to the buck in order to make a killing shot, because he carried only a bow and a quiver of arrows. By nature Caleb Masters was a quiet man, appreciating solitude and serenity, so he chose to hunt with a bow rather than a rifle.

Caleb was a squat built man about five foot four, with a husky chest, broad shoulders, and muscular arms and legs. He was dressed all in buckskin except for a beaver skin cap, and his face was covered with a heavy dark beard, so hunched down a bit he looked more like an animal than a man. The Cheyenne brave watching him studied this new creature with curiosity and caution.

Caleb became aware of the Indian, but carefully avoided making any movement that would display this knowledge. Experience with Kiowa and

Comanche Indians in Texas had taught him such wisdom, and had given him the ability to evade any pursuit.

Moving behind some thick cover, Caleb slipped out of sight down into a nearby gully. As he did so he startled a bear that was busy eating honey from a beehive. Caleb hurried through the gully away from both the bear and the Indian.

The Cheyenne watched the hunter step into the dense brush. Waiting for him to emerge on the other side, he was a bit startled when a bear ambled into view instead. The bear looked around, shook its head a few times, and then returned into the brush. It was several minutes later when the Cheyenne saw Caleb come into view again as he arrived at the distant end of the gully.

The next time Caleb was seen, it was by two Cheyenne braves. They watched him scrambling up into a rock basin. They wondered where he was going and what he was doing. They didn't realize that he had seen them, and was making his escape.

Caleb struggled over the rocks and boulders, staying beneath an overhang to remain hidden as he moved down into the valley below. He saw an eagle rise above and soar away.

The two Indians watched as Caleb disappeared into the boulders. Then they also saw the eagle

Many Shapes

as it glided in a wide circle and suddenly plunged downward into the brush and trees in the valley. A short time later they saw Caleb step out of the brush below carrying a turkey that he had shot.

These two incidents were discussed among the Cheyenne with great concern. The shaman spoke solemnly. Surely this hunter must be observed with much care.

Clever Fox was moving cautiously around a bend in the wash trying to get a better look at the hunter when the wolf hurled from the bank above and knocked him down. His head struck a rock and he was briefly unconscious.

Caleb was just stepping around the same bend from the other direction, when the wolf leaped. Using his bow as a club, he drove the animal away. Caleb knelt over the fallen Cheyenne to see what his condition was. As he did this, the Indian came awake.

In a partial daze, Clever Fox gazed up into Caleb's smiling face. What he saw was two piercing eyes and shining teeth. The terrified Cheyenne clawed his way backward, scrambled to his knees, jumped to his feet and rapidly ran away from Caleb.

This encounter established Caleb's legend. He became known as "Many Shapes". Had the Cheyenne not seen him change into a bear, and an eagle, and then a wolf? He was looked upon with great esteem and reverence.

Caleb never knew why the Cheyenne always remained at a distance whenever he saw them. After a while he became accustomed to their behavior, and was simply grateful. One fall Caleb got a hankering to go back home to Texas, and was never seen in Wyoming again.

The Cheyenne still talk of "Many Shapes". They remember exactly when he went away. That was the year the white buffalo was seen leaving with the herd.

THE LONG SHOT

Pete Smith and Zack Johnson gazed at the big buck deer from a distance. As usual they argued about which one of them was going to be able to shoot the deer.

Pete and Zack had roamed over the western plains and mountains together for more than forty years. They were normally great companions. But the one thing they could never agree on was whose shot brought down or would bring down any game they were after.

Smith wasn't really Pete's last name, and for that matter not actually his first either. He was born Peytor in the old country, with a last name no one could pronounce. So he was called Pete, and he took the name Smith just to make things easier.

Pete wasn't sure about Zack Johnson. Maybe he also had another name at one time. This was not an uncommon thing. He really didn't care. He and Zack were good pals. That was all that mattered.

Except for who was the better shot. That mattered. They had argued about this every since they first met. The arguing never led to much of anything except a lot of swearing and grumbling. And it never settled a dispute. Not one.

So with a big buck moving slowly through the brush in the wooded valley below they each moved quickly into position to get the first shot. Zack moved cautiously down the hill trying to get closer. Pete, anxious to get the first crack, knelt by an outcropping of rocks, and confidently readied for a longer shot.

The buck would stop hidden from sight, then slide into view for a few moments, and then quickly disappear again. Zack had cut the distance in half now, but didn't see the deer just then. But apparently Pete did, because Zack saw Pete throw his rifle to his shoulder. Zack searched the thick brush for any glimpse of the deer, and then he

The Long Shot

saw the buck move. It was still a long shot, he thought. He should probably be trying to get even closer. But neither would let the other win. Both rifles barked. The deer dropped as if pole axed.

"Yeow," cried out Pete. "I sure nailed that critter."

"No ya didn't," shouted Zack. "It was me that downed that buck."

"Don't talk foolish, Zack. Even as close as you was, ya know ya couldn't make that shot!"

"Well, I sure as hell just did, you cussed old varmint. It was my shot that did the trick."

"No it wasn't, dangit. I shot first and felled that deer afore you was even ready ta pull the trigger," shouted Pete.

The two old timers shuffled down the hill to where the deer was laying. They continued arguing all the way. Pete stopped once and jump up and down, stomping his feet like a little kid. Zack shook his fist in Pete's face to emphasize his position.

Neither man would give in, even though forty years of wrangling like this never arrived at any agreement.

When they got to the deer, they were startled to find a young fellow sitting against a tree a short distance on the other side of the buck.

"You gents sure do make a lot of noise, bellowing like you do," said the younger man.

"Gee-haus-afat," exclaimed Pete loudly. "Whaterya doin' sittin' there?"

"I been waitin' for you. You musta been a long way off when you shot, since you been some time getting' here."

"Yeah, I reckon it was close to four hundred yards," blustered Pete proudly.

"Mighty long way," murmured the younger fellow shaking his head. "A mighty long way."

"Where in tarnation did ya come from?" asked Zack.

"Well I was sneakin' up on this buck from back behind me, opposite of where you was, when you up and shot him. Looks like you beat me to it, don't it!"

"Yeah! I made a really great shot," boasted Pete triumphantly.

"Ya never did no such thing," yelled Zack "I shot him!"

"Seems you gentlemen have some difference of opinion," chuckled the young man. "I could hear you arguing comin' all the way down the hill."

"This here obstinate old coon just won't admit that I shot this deer," said Zack.

"Well, now maybe I can shed some light on your question," said the young hunter.

The Long Shot

"And just how was ya ta be doin' that?" growled Pete.

"I was down here sneakin' up close to make my own try at the deer when I heard the two shots. They was close together, but one was just a hair ahead. Who shot first?"

"He did," mumbled Zack pointing to Pete.

"Ya bet yer sweet petooties I did," snorted Pete.

Well, then I can say with certainty it's your bullet in that deer, Mister." The young fellow pointed at Zack.

"And just where do ya think my bullet is?" groused Pete sarcastically.

The younger man looked at Pete and calmly said, "Why it's right here in my arm."

ONE GOOD TURN

Burned out of their homes near Clinton, Missouri by the Kansas Missouri raiders shortly after Lee's surrender, the McClellan brothers, George and Adam, decided to move their families west to Oklahoma Territory. They figured since they would have to start all over anyway, they might do better in a new place.

They were able to acquire two covered wagons, and two teams of horses to pull them, at a sum they could afford. With their wives, Betsy and June, and their children, Michael, Thomas, and Sally, they packed up what meager belongings they could salvage, and started west. Trailing behind the second wagon on tethers were two milk cows and four steers.

George and Adam each rode a chestnut gelding. The trail was hot and dusty in Kansas, but the women never complained, and the children thought it was a great adventure.

A couple of days after crossing the border, the McClellan's met a Union Cavalry patrol from Fort Leavenworth. Lieutenant Avery Parsons, introduced himself. Asking about their destination and learning where they were bound, he advised that they hire a guide.

"Where might we find one," asked Adam.

"Well, Isaiah Longbow is a good scout when he has a mind to it," replied Parsons. "He's got a cabin just over that little hill you can see yonder."

The lieutenant paused and then remarked, "He's part Indian and knows this country like the back of his hand."

The lieutenant chuckled. "Course he might be drunk."

"I'm not sure it would be wise to hire a drunken guide," said George.

Parsons laughed. "Longbow is reliable when he's guiding. He takes guiding very seriously, so he doesn't drink then. But when he's not guiding, then he takes drinking very seriously."

"It wouldn't do any harm to talk to him, George," said Adam. "A guide might be a smart idea."

George nodded. "Yeah, I spose you're right." He thanked the officer for his advice and information, and the two groups went their separate ways.

The McClellans were pleasantly surprised when they met Isaiah Longbow. His face was cleanly shaven, his hair was long but well groomed, and his buckskin clothing although worn was clean. Best of all he was sober.

One Good Turn

"I bin kinda itchin' ta hit the trail agin," chuckled Longbow. "Bin drinkin' steady for a while, but it's got long in the tooth. Right happy you stopped by."

So just like that, the McClellans had a guide. Longbow knew where they could find water when it was needed. He always managed to find a well sheltered spot to camp. He was an excellent marksman with his old Spencer, and provided meat regularly.

Longbow guided the McClellans around the big cities like Topeka and Wichita. "Them is wild and dangerous places we'd best avoid."

He said, "When we got to get more supplies we can buy them in the smaller towns. The store keepers there will be more friendly and a heap more honest."

So they moved south westerly into Oklahoma Territory without much incident.

Once there Longbow took on a more cautious demeanor. And it was his Indian savvy, that proved to be mighty beneficial one evening. Betsy and June shrieked at the same time as a group of eight Indians suddenly appeared on a nearby hill.

"Kiowas," said Longbow calmly. "Looks to be huntin' party. They ain't painted for war." He carefully picked up his Spencer. "That don't mean we shouldn't be careful."

Longbow watched as the Kiowas slowly rode closer. Then they stopped and just sat watching the whitemen.

"They got their eye on yer cows," said the guide. "They'll likely try ta steal one. Mebbe not right now. Most likely later tonight."

"What do you think we should do?" asked George.

Holding up his rifle Adam said, "Looks like they only have bows. We can shoot a couple if they try to steal our cows. Our guns should scare them off."

"That might work ifin they was the only Indians around. But this small huntin' party is probably from a bigger bunch. We shoot a couple of these, and we most like got a real hot fight on our hands," said Longbow

"So you think we should just let them steal one of our cows?" asked George.

"No, I got a better idea," replied Longbow. "If we let **them** take one, they might run off with one a yer milk cows. But if **we give** em one, we kin choose a steer."

"I guess that kind of makes sense," said Adam. "How do we go about doing it?"

"Well, this may sound a bit crazy, but I reckon one of yer ladies should do it. Them Kiowas won't

One Good Turn

get too excited ifin a woman was to walk out there toward them. She could lead one of yer steers, and then just leave it there, and come back here."

"You really are crazy!" bellowed Adam. "We are not going to allow one of our wives to put herself in that kind of danger."

"I'll do it," said Betsy quietly. Before George could object, she said again, "I'll do it. Now, George, don't get all worked up over a simple thing like this. Mister Longbow has been right about everything up 'til now. I don't see any reason to question his good judgment in this case."

With that, Betsy calmly walked over to where the cattle were tethered, and selected one of the steers. She showed no sign of fear as she led the animal away from the wagons toward the Indians. A little over halfway she stopped and untied the steer. She turned her back to the Kiowas and slowly returned to her family.

The Kiowas sat unmoving and watched as the woman walked from the wagons leading the steer. They waited a few minutes after she left, and then one of the braves slid off his pony and went to the steer. He put a rope around the animals neck, and started back to his companions. He stopped for a moment. Looking back at the wagons he waved a hand in friendly gesture. When he reached the other Kiowas, he mounted his pony and the eight braves rode away with the steer.

The next afternoon, while Isaiah Longbow was out scouting, four horsemen, rough in appearance and heavily armed, approached the two McClellan wagons. They made no immediate menacing gestures.

Both George and Adam held their rifles across their chests, and studied the four men as they stopped about twenty feet away.

"Kinda surprised ta find white folks out here in the middle of nowhere," spoke up one of the four. "Where ya bound fer?"

"Don't rightly know just yet," answered George. "Guess we'll know when we get there."

"Ya wouldn't happen ta have a cup of coffee you'd spare?" asked another man.

"I guess we could do that," said Adam.

"There's a bunch of wild Kiowas runnin' around near here. We had a set-to with 'em a ways back. Maybe we should join up with you fer awhile. Some extra guns just might be handy if they should decide ta jump you."

Betsy was about to say something of their recent encounter, but George shook his head with a warning look.

Just then Isaiah Longbow rode up. As he dismounted, he carefully looked over the four strangers.

"You boys figure on ta settle in here fer awhile?" asked Longbow.

"They offered to help protect us from the Kiowas," remarked George.

"Did they now? Well, that's down right neighborly." The guide strolled over and helped himself to a cup of coffee. He poured a second cup and carried it over to George.

In a low voice he said, "Might be better ta have em here where we kin watch em. Chase em away and they might come back shootin' after dark. Mebbe if we act hospitable they'll just ride away. It ain't likely, but we kin hope."

Longbow turned back to the four men. "I reckon ya might as well get off them tired horses, an make yerself comfortable." He watched as they dismounted, and made note that didn't indicate any intent to unsaddle their animals.

The four strangers nodded to one another and moving separately took four commanding positions. Suddenly drawing revolvers they threatened the McClellan group. "Don't do anything foolish," said the man who seemed to be the leader. "We don't aim ta kill ya if it ain't necessary. We're just gonna take yer guns and horses, and also some food. And of course any money you might happen ta have."

"Can we take the women with us, Cliff?" asked one of the other men.

"We just might do that!"

The words were barely out of the leader's mouth when an arrow buried into his chest. Almost at the same time each of the other robbers were struck solidly by killing arrows.

As quickly as the attack had begun, it stopped abruptly. No more arrows were forthcoming. Then suddenly a Kiowa brave appeared. It was the same brave who had led the steer away. He stepped over to where the dead men lay. He looked at each man very carefully, and then knelt down over one.

The McClellans and Longbow watched as the Kiowa drew his knife. It appeared he was going to scalp the dead man. Betsy and June looked away. But instead, the Kiowa cut a leather thong from around the dead man's neck. He stood and held up a silver ornament.

The Kiowa walked over to Betsy. "Was my woman's," he said solemnly. Then he pressed the ornament into Betsy's hand and nodded. He whirled about quickly and was gone.

MUSICAL RENDERINGS

Come, tighten your girth
and slacken your rein;
Come, buckle your blanket
and holster again;
Try the click of your trigger
and balance your blade,
For he must ride sure
that goes Riding a Raid!

These words rang out boisterously in the Confederate camp outside of Bowling Green, Kentucky. Matthew Savage and his sister, Cora Belle, were entertaining the troops, and the soldiers had spontaneously joined in the song.

Matt, who played guitar, was dressed in pin stripped black pants and a ruffled black shirt covered with a fancy gold vest. Cora Belle sang and danced wearing a bright red saloon girl's dress that complimented her fiery colored hair. She had a dazzling smile and a laugh that beguiled the men in grey.

Cora Belle and Matt both had fine singing voices and harmonized well on many favorite songs such as "Dixie", and "The Bonnie Blue Flag" or "The Yellow Rose of Texas".

> *Oh, yes, I am a Southern girl,*
> *And glory in the name.*
> *And boast it with far greater pride*
> *than glitring wealth or fame.*

Cora Belle sang this song with gusto as she paraded through the Confederate troops with flashing eyes and flirtatious moves. The men in grey applauded wildly and cheered with enthusiansm.

Music was playing an important role in the Civil War. Composers like Root and Work in the North, and Blackmar and Hewitt in the South published a phenomenal number of songs that both the soldiers and the folks back home found to be inspirational and pleasing.

Matt and Cora Belle were two of several wandering minstrels that visited camp after camp singing and dancing. The troops all welcomed them and enjoyed these entertaining moments.

> *A hundred months have passed, Lorena,*
> *Since last I held your hand in mine.*
> *And felt the pulse beat fast, Lorena,*
> *Though mine beat faster far than thine.*

This love song, a favorite of the soldiers, brought tears to the eyes of the men in grey camped beside the Duck River.

Musical Renderings

Then Matt and Cora Belle livened things up with a hearty rendition of "Goober Peas", a jovial comic song supposedly written by A. Pindar. Esq and P. Nutt. Esq. Goober and Pindar being slang words meaning peanut.

Matt had numerous sheets of music that he carried with him from camp to camp. Some of these contained original written scores. When the two siblings weren't actually performing they moved about the camps talking to the soldiers. And sometimes these conversations became the basis for the musical notes Matt was writing.

All quiet along the Potomac tonight,

Except here and there a stray picket

Is shot, as he walks his beat to and fro,

By a rifleman hid in the thicket.

Although the words depicted a somber and mournful situation, the Confederate soldiers camped along the Tennessee River cheered when Matt and Cora Belle sang this song. Perhaps it was because they felt that the song represented a peril that each of them shared.

Matt and Cora Belle moved on to another Confederate camp. And then another and yet another. By now the sheet music that Matt was writing was developing into a substantial packet. There were a couple of times that Confederate officers had been curious about his scribbling. When he showed them his wordless musical compositions dispersed among a group of published songs, they smiled and walked away.

Not too long after, Matt and Cora Belle journeyed North to Camp Buell where Matt turned over his music to Colonel Minor Millikin a Union Army intelligence officer.

The original scores had no meaning to any musician. They were intended to be translated by telegraphers. Quarter notes represented dashes and the eighth notes dots. Various other musical notations such as whole notes, half notes, rests and bars separated words written in Morse code. These messages contained Confederate locations, troop numbers, armaments, supply statistics, and other useful information.

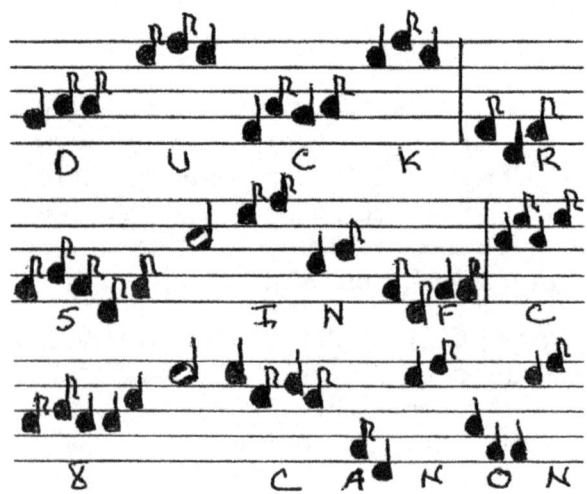

Musical renderings to help the Union.

LEGERDEMAIN

Joe Bradford was playing with some children in front of his office. They were mesmerized as he did a few clever tricks for their entertainment. Simple things like making a coin that he was holding vanish, and then reappear behind one of the lad's ear. Or making a slim piece of paper seem to float above his hand.

Joe was the sheriff of Peyote, New Mexico. A slim man of forty-eight, with bright eyes and nimble fingers, he enjoyed performing for the boys and girls who eagerly crowded around him.

Peyote was a quiet town with a dreamlike spirit about it that perhaps accounted for its name. Joe liked it that way and hoped to keep the citizens of his peaceful town happy and safe.

Today was much like every other day had been for the past couple of years. The townsfolk passing by the sheriffs office nodded or waved to Joe as he did his daily magic show. Joe smiled and waved back whenever it didn't interfere with one of his tricks.

The children always encouraged him by laughing and applauding. Joe was sure that at least one or two had figured out a couple of his easier tricks, but they never let on. The slight-of-hand he was about to perform was his best.

Joe took a small plain paper bag out of his shirt pocket and unfolded it. He opened the bag and shook it several times as he turned it upside down, to show that the bag was empty. Then he held it out to the children so they could look into it for further assurance that the bag was indeed empty.

Next Joe opened each of his hands, shifting the bag from one to the other, to show that he wasn't holding anything except the bag.

Now holding the empty bag in his right hand, Joe reached down with his left hand and closed his fingers as if picking up an object that the children could see was clearly not there.

The children's heads all looked up as Joe's left hand made a tossing motion into the air. Their eyes followed his right hand as he moved the bag around as if trying to catch whatever he had tossed. But there was nothing in sight to catch.

Then to their amazement, they saw the bag jerk and heard the sound of something falling into the bag. Joe smiled, and asked a little girl to hold out her hand. As she did so, he turned the bag upside down over her hand and shook it. But nothing fell out.

Joe peered into the bag, and then looked at the children with a puzzled expression. They watched him very carefully as he reached into the bag with his left hand and seemed to take out something.

Legerdemain

Joe again made a tossing motion with his left hand, and again the children's heads followed, and again they didn't see anything up in the air. Again Joe moved the bag around as if trying to catch something, and just as before, the children saw the bag jerk and heard something fall into the bag.

When Joe emptied the bag into the little girls hand this time, still nothing came out. Once more Joe looked puzzled and peered into the bag. Then he said, "I must not be grabbing what's in the bag correctly." He smiled at the little girl. "Why don't you reach into the bag and toss what ever is in there up into the air."

A lot of the children had seen Joe do this trick before and knew just what to expect. They had never figured out how it was done, and so they watched anxiously.

The little girl reached into the bag and felt around. Joe said, "Close your hand, take it out of the bag, and make a tossing motion into the air."

The girl did as she was told, and once more Joe made a motion with the bag to catch what could not be seen. And once more the children saw the bag jerk and heard the sound of something falling into the bag.

"Hold out your hand," said Joe to the little girl. This time when the bag was held upside down and shaken several pieces of candy fell into the girls hand.

The children cheered and laughed. Of course they had seen this trick many times before, and especially delighted in getting the candy. Joe grinned. He was always pleased to be able to bring so much happiness to them.

"That's a very clever trick, Sheriff." The words sounded harsh as they came from across the street. "It's too bad you won't be able to do it again!" Joe looked in the direction of the snarling voice.

"You remember me, Bradford?"

Joe recognized Mace Steele. Joe had arrested Steele a few years back. "I thought you were in Yuma prison," said Joe.

"I broke out," replied Steele who was standing about fifty feet away. "I told you I'd get even for you sending me to Yuma."

Joe carefully folded the paper bag and slid it into his shirt pocket. As he did so, he slowly started to walk toward Mace Steele. With his left hand Joe grasped the edge of his jacket and held it open, as his right hand settled on the handle of a knife that was in the sheath hanging from his belt. He continued to walk toward Steele while he removed the knife from the sheath.

Steele burst out laughing. "You really are one dumb lawman, bringing a knife to a gunfight," snarled the killer as he pulled his Colt from its holster and pointed it at Joe.

"Well, a man uses whatever he's got," replied Joe continuing to walk.

"That's a mighty wicked looking knife, I gotta admit." said Steele. "You don't seriously think I'm gonna let you get close enough to me to use it?"

Joe made a couple of slashing moves with the knife, like one would with a sword. He had closed the distance to about twelve feet. As he was making another slashing motion two gun shots exploded. The first shot smashed Mace Steele's gun hand. The second tore up his right knee cap.

As Mace Steele lay writhing in pain in the street, Sheriff Bradford stood over him. "It appears that you're going back to Yuma, Mace. Bringing a knife to a gunfight worked just fine. You were so busy watching the blade flash, you didn't see me slide my left hand into my jacket pocket where I keep a twenty-five caliber. It's something called *misdirection!*"

PRINTS

An incident occurred many years ago while I was deer hunting with my pal, Danny Martin, that has had me wondering and baffled ever since. It's not something I dwell on, but every once in a while it nags at me.

Danny and I did a lot of fishing and hunting together. Those were really great times, and have produced some fantastic stories. I know that everyone thinks stretching a yarn is common among fishermen and hunters. But sometimes what sounds like a tall tale is the God's own truth.

Anyway, this one summer Danny and I decided that in preparation for fall hunting we would build us a cabin up in the foot hills so we could 'camp in style'. Fall is the best time to find plump deer fattened up by the summer grasses and other feed.

When it was finished, the cabin wasn't much more than a shack. But it did have a roof of some sorts and a door that could be closed and barred shut from the inside. We did have to use home made sleeping bags to keep warm at night. But still it was shelter from wind and rain.

Well, this one night we were tucked in after a days hunting that produced no deer but had left us mighty tired. We grabbed a bite to eat. Some sandwiches we had thought to bring with. Slugged down some hot coffee, and hit the hay.

Just before we fell asleep it started to snow. Not a storm, but just enough to cover the ground. We looked forward to hunting in the morning now, since the snow would make it easier to track deer.

Danny was snoring before I fell asleep, but I was tired enough so it didn't keep me awake. Sometime in the middle of the night I was awakened by a rustling sound from outside our shack. I listened for a few minutes and then shut my eyes to sleep some more.

I'm not sure how much later it was when I realized that the sound from outside was still going on.

Danny wasn't snoring anymore, so I asked, "Hey, Danny, are you awake?"

He whispered back, "Yeah."

"Do you hear that strange rustling sound outside?" I asked him.

"Yeah, I been listenin' to it for a while."

We both lay there quietly. Then Danny said, "What do ya think it is?"

"I haven't the foggiest idea," I replied.

"Me neither," he answered.

Prints

We both lay there listening some more. "It sounds like it's bigger than a coon or skunk. Ya think it might be a bear?" Danny asked.

"No it don't seem to be that big. Could be a small deer, I suppose,"

"Do ya think we should get up and look outside?" he asked.

"What ever it is, it don't seem to be tryin' ta get inside the shack. We got our rifles in here if it does try. Let's just go back ta sleep and wait 'til morning to look around," I said.

Come dawn the sound outside had stopped. Danny and I both lay still listening to make sure. All was quiet.

We both rolled out of our sleeping bags and stretched. We didn't have to dress 'cause we had slept in our clothes. We eased over to the door, opened it slowly and peered out.

We didn't see any animals. What we did see really surprised and confused us. Foot prints in the fresh snow. Little cowboy boots, like a ladies or a young child. They circled the shack going in both directions several times. The prints didn't approach the shack at any point, staying about six feet away all around.

The really strange thing was that there were no prints leading into or going away from the circle of tracks surrounding the shack.

Also by James J. Huble

APPEARANCES

A Collection of
16 Western Short Stories
ISBN# 978-0-9825963-7-1

TWISTED TRAILS

A Collection of
18 Western Short Stories
each with a 'Twist'
ISBN# 978-1-939345-04-2

Available from
Goose Flats Publishing
P.O. Box 813
Tombstone, Arizona, 85638
www.gooseflats.com

Amazon.com

BarnesAndNoble.com

and from the Author.

Dealer inquiries welcomed

About the Author

James Huble is retired and lives in the Catalina foothills north of Tucson Arizona. He taught English, speech, dramatics, and philosophy; is a published poet and a song writer, and has performed professionally as a musician and actor. When writing these  short stories, you might say he assumed the role of a chuck wagon cook; rustling up a pot full of situations, stirring in a little theatrical flavor, and seasoning with a mischievous perspective.

CPSIA information can be obtained
at www.ICGtesting.com
Printed in the USA
LVHW020112021220
673182LV00043B/1191